TEENAGE MUTANT NINJA TURTLES

NEW ANIMATED ADVENTURES

VOLUME 3

STORY: SCOTT TIPTON & DAVID TIPTON

SCRIPT: SCOTT TIPTON, DAVID TIPTON WITH KENNY BYERLY

ART: DARIO BRIZUELA

COLORS: HEATHER BRECKEL

LETTERS: SHAWN LEE

EDITS: BOBBY CURNOW

ABDOPUBLISHING.COM

Reinforced library bound edition published in 2016 by Spotlight, a division of ABDO
PO Box 398166, Minneapolis, Minnesota 55439. Spotlight produces high-quality
reinforced library bound editions for schools and libraries.
Published by agreement with IDW.

Printed in the United States of America, North Mankato, Minnesota.
092015
012016

THIS BOOK CONTAINS
RECYCLED MATERIALS

CATALOGING-IN-PUBLICATION DATA

Byerly, Kenny.
 Teenage Mutant Ninja Turtles : new animated adventures / writer, Kenny Byerly ; illustrator, Dario
Brizuela. -- Reinforced library bound edition.
   p. cm. (Teenage Mutant Ninja Turtles : new animated adventures)
Volumes 1-2 written by Kenny Byerly ; illustrated by Dario Brizuela. -- Volume 3 written by Scott
Tipton, David Tipton, and Kenny Byerly ; illustrated by Dario Brizuela. -- Volume 4 written by Erik
Burnham ; illustrated by Dario Brizuela.
Summary: Spinning straight out of the hit Nickelodeon show, a fantastic tale takes the Turtles on a
dangerous rescue mission.
ISBN 978-1-61479-459-2 (vol. 1) -- ISBN 978-1-61479-460-8 (vol. 2) -- ISBN 978-1-61479-461-5
(vol. 3) -- ISBN 978-1-61479-462-2 (vol. 4)
1. Teenage Mutant Ninja Turtles (Fictitious characters)--Juvenile fiction.
2. Superheroes--Juvenile fiction. 3. Adventure and adventurers--Juvenile fiction. 4. Graphic
novels--Juvenile fiction. I. Brizuela, Dario, illustrator. II. Tipton, Scott, author. III. Tipton, David,
author. IV. Burnham, Erik, author. V. Title.
741.5--dc23
                    2015955128

Spotlight

A Division of ABDO
abdopublishing.com

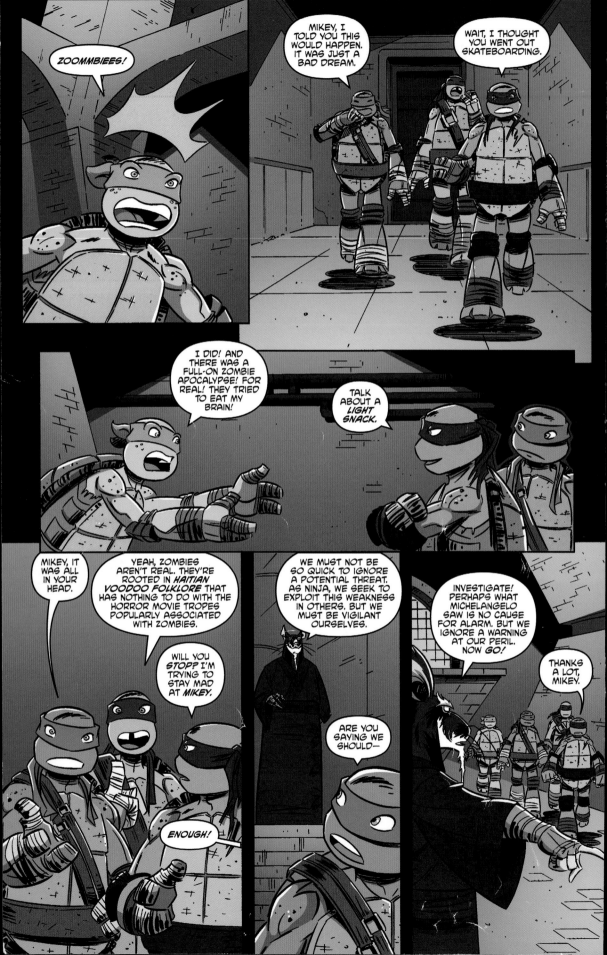

SLEEP RESEARCH INSTITUTE

TOLD YOU THIS WAS BIG.

OK, I ADMIT THERE'S SOMETHING GOING ON HERE. BUT I DON'T THINK THESE ARE EXACTLY ZOMBIES, MIKEY.

THEN THEY'RE *INFECTED MUTANTS* LIKE IN THAT MOVIE *TOXIC TOMORROW!*

MIKEY, UNCOOL. WE'RE MUTANTS.

RIIIIGHT.

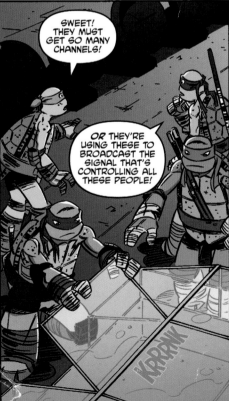

SWEET! THEY MUST GET SO MANY CHANNELS!

OR THEY'RE USING THESE TO BROADCAST THE SIGNAL THAT'S CONTROLLING ALL THESE PEOPLE!

KRRRNK

WHOAAAA...

WHAT EXACTLY WERE YOU WORKING ON HERE, ANNIE?

I WAS DEVELOPING REMOTE BRAIN SCANNING TECHNOLOGY TO RECREATE PEOPLE'S DREAMS. BUT THE KRAANG MADE ME USE MY RESEARCH TO *CONTROL* PEOPLE'S DREAMS, AND FROM THERE, TO CONTROL SLEEPING *PEOPLE*.

THEY FORCED ME TO BUILD THAT *THING* OUT THERE.

NOW THEY WANT TO USE MY "DREAM MACHINE" AS A MODEL TO BUILD AN EVEN BIGGER ONE. THEY'LL BE ABLE TO CONTROL THE WHOLE CITY!

SEE? WE GOTTA SMASH IT!

THAT COULD DAMAGE THE SLEEPWALKERS' BRAINS. IT'D BE LIKE DISCONNECTING A DRIVE FROM YOUR COMPUTER WITHOUT EJECTING IT.

HA! SEE?

I DON'T SUPPOSE YOU BUILT AN OFF SWITCH?

THEY DIDN'T WANT ME TO AND THEY NEVER LEFT ME ALONE WITH THE MACHINE, BUT I FIGURED OUT A WAY.

THIS PROGRAM WILL SAFELY WAKE EVERYONE UP, THEN TRIGGER A SELF-DESTRUCT SEQUENCE.

PERFECT.

JUST PLUG IT IN AND IT DOES THE REST. BUT MAKE SURE YOU GET EVERYONE OUT. THE SELF-DESTRUCT PART COULD GET... EXPLODE-Y.

GOT IT. OH, AND, UH—YOU NEVER SAW US, OKAY? WE'RE KINDA NOT SUPPOSED TO LET PEOPLE KNOW WE EXIST.

YEAH, WELL, I WASN'T REALLY SUPPOSED TO HELP ALIENS ENSLAVE A BUNCH OF NEW YORKERS, EITHER. YOUR SECRET'S SAFE WITH ME.

RUN? LOOK HOW SLOW THEY ARE! THEY *STILL* HAVEN'T GOTTEN TO US!

SO IF WE CAN'T HIT THEM, THEN WHAT?

THEY DON'T SEEM TO BE DOING MUCH...

I THINK WE CAN JUST PUSH THROUGH WITHOUT HURTING THEM.

HA! GET AROUND *THAT*, SORTA-ZOMBIE-DUDE!

EXCUSE ME, COMING THROUGH!

URK!

KRAANGDROIDS IN THE CROWD!

KLAANG

TELL HER YOURSELF, BRO!

THWOP

'CAUSE THAT WAS GETTING TOO LONG TO REMEMBER ANYWAY.

I TOLD YOU GUYS! YOU CAN'T JUST WALK INTO A ZOMBIE HORDE!

YOU GOTTA STAY ON THE MOVE!

THE GOOD THING ABOUT ZOMBIES IS THEY DON'T CLIMB.

AW MAN! THEY BREAK ALL THE RULES!

RATTLE RATTLE

BZZZT

BWOOP BWOOP BWOOP

HE DID IT!

NOW WE'VE GOTTA GET THESE PEOPLE OUT OF HERE!

KRAANG MUST STOP THE STOPPING OF THE PLAN THAT IS IMPORTANT TO KRAANG! UNPLUG THE DEVICE USED BY THE ONES WHO ARE CALLED THE TURTLES!

HEY ZOMBIE SLEEPWALKER WHATEVERS! OVER HERE!

COME ON, HURRY UP! I WISH THEY WERE THOSE FAST ZOMBIES.

WHAT'S GOING ON?

WHERE AM I?

WHAT HAPPENED?

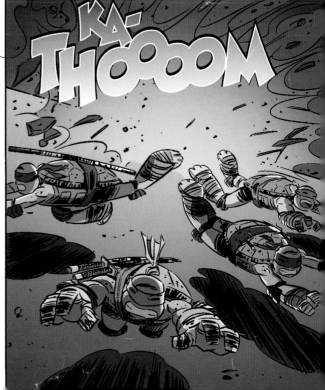